GYNORMOUS!

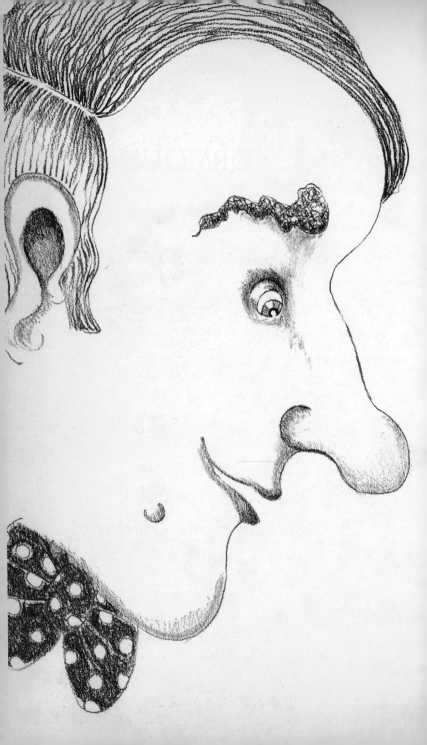

GYNORMOUS!
The Ultimate Book of Giants

Adrian Mitchell
Illustrated by Sally Gardner

Orion Children's Books
and
Dolphin Paperbacks

First published in Great Britain in 1996
Published in paperback in 1996
by Orion Children's Books
a division of the Orion Publishing Group Ltd
Orion House
5 Upper St Martin's Lane
London WC2H 9EA

A catalogue record for this book is
available from the British Library
Printed in Great Britain
ISBN 1 85881 150 3 (HB)
ISBN 1 85881 302 6 (PB)

*For seven years I battled against
a mighty giant with fair hair and terrible
fists. I was two years four days young than
him. He was my older brother Jimmy. But
after seven years of warfare we made a
kind of peace. And after seven years
of peace we became great friends.
And now I am about as tall as he is,
I dedicate this book,
with love, to Jimmy.*

Contents

Introduction   9

What to do when you meet a Giant   10

The Zimwi and the Singing Drum
(a Swahili story)   12

David and Goliath Rap   18

Don Quixote and the Windmill Giants
(a Spanish story by Cervantes)   24

The Giant's Love Song   30

The Sad Boy who Conquered the Giants
(a story from Canada)   32

I am Boj   46

The Haunted Well
(a story from the Punjab)   48

At Midnight   58

Bala of the Golden Lake   60

The Sadness of a Giant Child   68

Seven at a Blow   70

Threatening   83

The Playful Giant of Carn Galva   84

The Flying Giants   88

Simpkin Smallstuff and the Starmaiden   90

Hairy Giants   95

Introduction

In my long, long life I have met many very tall people. Every one of them was kind, gentle and intelligent. (Well, one was a bully for a couple of years, but then he gave it up and devoted the rest of his life to helping the helpless.)

So I'm not afraid of big people. The sad fact is that in most stories giants are wicked ogres who eat little children and are tricked and often killed. I've included some of those because they are such great stories. But this book also hopes to introduce you to some good friends who happen to be ten times your size.

Adrian Mitchell

WHAT TO DO WHEN YOU MEET A GIANT

Don't shout out Wow! then stand and stare
Don't try to sit upon his chair
Don't ask him if it's cold up there
Don't ask if he liked Giant Despair
In John Bunyan's *Pilgrim's Progress*
Don't use the words Ogre or Ogress
Don't ask him if he'd like a snack
Or mention Beanstalks, David, Jack
Or even Snow White and the Seven -
Or say "You're very near to heaven"
Just be yourself and, in the end,
You may have made your greatest friend.

The Zimwi and the Singing Drum

Some girls were gathering seashells on the beach. One of them picked up a specially fine cowrie shell, which she was afraid of losing, so she put it carefully on a rock.

When it was time to go home, she forgot the shell, and only remembered it later. Nobody would come with her, so she walked back alone to collect the cowrie, singing to herself.

She found a Zimwi, who is a magical giant, sitting on the rock. He said to the girl: "Come closer, I can't hear what you're saying."

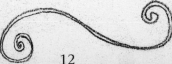

She came nearer to him, singing:

"The sun lies down.
 The red waves swell.
Let me come and take
 My cowrie shell."

But he said: "Come a little closer, I still can't hear you." She took another step towards him, and another, and then he reached out and grabbed her and put her into the drum he carried and fastened down the drumskin with the girl inside.

Then he strutted about from village to village. Whenever he beat the drum, the girl inside it sang with such a sweet voice that everybody marvelled. At last he came to the girl's own village, where the people begged him to beat his drum and sing.

He asked for some beer, and when it was brought, he beat his drum. But when the girl began to sing so sweetly, her parents

recognized the voice of their own child.

So they gave the Zimwi more and more beer until it sent him to sleep. Then they opened his drum and freed their daughter. They put some bees and biting ants and a snake into the drum and fastened down the drumskin again.

Then they woke up the Zimwi and told him some people from the next village had arrived and wanted to hear the singing drum. But the drum just made an awful buzzing and hissing noise.

The Zimwi sat down and opened it to see what was wrong. But as soon as he opened it, the snake jumped out and bit his nose and he died.

Now on the spot where the Zimwi died a pumpkin began to grow. And it grew and it grew until some children were walking past and said: "What a fine big pumpkin! Let's get father's sword and split it open!"

But the pumpkin became very angry and chased the children. They ran and ran till they came to a river and an old ferryman took them across, but the terrible pumpkin rolled its way over the river and after them.

The children found some men in a village and shouted out: "Hide us from that

pumpkin! The Zimwi has turned into a
pumpkin and he's chasing us. When it
comes, take it and burn it with fire." So the
men hid the children under some blankets.

The pumpkin came rolling into the village
and it said to the men: "Have you seen my
runaway slaves pass this way?"

"What sort of slaves?" asked the men. "We
haven't seen any slaves."

"That's a lie," said the pumpkin. "You've
hidden them under those blankets."

But the men grabbed the pumpkin and
put it on the fire and burned it to ashes
and threw the ashes away on the wind.
Then the children came out from
under their blankets and
the men took
them safely
home to
their mothers.

DAVID AND GOLIATH RAP

Once upon a time there was a terrible war -
Though no one ever told me what the war was for -
But the army of the Philistine was hot for a fight,
And so was the army of the Israelite.

They shouted at each other, they hollered and cursed
But nobody wanted to charge in first
When a Philistine giant stepped from the front rank,
With a ton of brass armour going clank clank clank.

He was eleven feet high and so was his spear.
He yelled: "My name's Goliath, and I've come here
To ask you to send me a man to fight -
Come on - feed me an Israelite."

But none of the Israelites fancied a tussle
With eleven foot of blood bone brass and muscle
Till a kid called David says: "I know about giants,
They can always be beaten by a little bit of science."

The King of Israel says: "Forget it son,
He weighs ten ton, you'll be out in round one."
David says: "I can take him, OK?"
King Saul says: "Who are you, anyway?"

"I'm just a shepherd boy, but I guard my flock
With a wicked little sling that I load with rock.
Every one of the slings I've slung were aces -
I can hit a wolf's nose at a thousand paces.

"I smashed up a lion and demolished a bear
And I'll do just the same to that hulk over there."
David grinned and the King gave a sigh
And said: "You've got the guts, boy, give it a try."

David takes a staff and he goes to look
For five smooth pebbles from a nearby brook
Then he calls out: "Goliath, you're in for a shock."
And Goliath replieth: "I'm ready to rock."

When Goliath sees David he cackles: "Little boy,
I'm going to shake you and break you like a baby's toy,
I'll crack your every bone from your skull to your toes
And I'll feed what's left to the jackals and crows."

All the Israelite army shudders with fear
When Goliath gives a roar and lifts his mighty spear
And the shadow of the giant falls cold on the land -
But David just smiles as he takes his stand

And he takes one pebble and pops it in his sling
And he slings that sling in a circling ring
And he slings that sling and he lets go - now!
And there's a pebble sunk deep into Goliath's brow.

For a moment there's a look of terrible surprise
Which lights up both of that giant's eyes,
Then the lights go out and Goliath is dead
With his face in the dust and a stone in his head.

So that's a happy ending for old King Saul
And the army of Israel and most of all
For little David with his cunning sling -
And that shepherd boy grew up to be King.

But when Goliath's mother read the *Palestine Post*
And learned how her loving son gave up the ghost,
Her great tears flooded the wilderness
And the whole world shook at the grief of a giantess.

Don Quixote and the Windmill Giants

Don Quixote was an elderly Spanish gentleman with a sad face. He read a great many romantic stories about the adventures of knights in the olden days. So he put on a suit of armour and set out on his horse Rosinante to rescue maidens in distress. With him he took his servant, Sancho Panza, who had never read any romantic stories and thought his master was kind but crazy. Many British people pronounce Don Quixote as Don Quick-Zot, but he would rather be Donkey Oatey. This is one of his adventures.

Don Quixote and Sancho Panza were riding along when they saw thirty or forty windmills.

"We're in luck," said Don Quixote. "Look at those thirty or forty monstrous giants. I will do battle with them and kill them all and we'll take all their treasure and be rich and God will be pleased to have such wicked creatures wiped off the face of the earth."

"What giants? Where?" said Sancho.

"Over there, up there, on that hill. Giants with horrible long arms. I have read in books that many giants have arms over six miles long."

"Now hang on, sir," said Sancho. "Those aren't giants. They're windmills. Those aren't arms. They're sails, sails whirling round in the wind. Like they're meant to. Right?"

"It is quite clear," said Don Quixote, "that you know nothing about high adventure. These are giants if ever I saw any. If you are scared, run away and say your prayers. I will advance and engage these thirty or forty in a ferocious and unequal battle."

He dug his spurs into his horse Rosinante, crying out at the top of his voice: "Stay and fight me, you great brutes. There is only one of me."

At this moment a wind arose, and the great sails of the windmills began to turn.

"Don't you wave your arms at me," he shouted. "I'm a knight and you can't frighten me."

He held up his shield, pointed his lance at the windmills and charged at full gallop. He pushed his lance right into the sail of the nearest windmill.

But the wind turned the sail so violently that it broke his lance to pieces. Rosinante was dragged to one side, and Don Quixote fell off, rolling painfully down the hill.

Sancho Panza rushed to help him. "I warned you, didn't I sir," he said. "They're only windmills. Nobody could take them for giants unless they had giants on the brain."

Don Quixote sat up carefully. "Do you
take me for a fool? Of course I know a
windmill when I see one. My enemies
wanted to rob me of the glory of killing the
giants. So they turned the giants into
windmills. It's obvious."

"If you say so, sir," said Sancho, helping
his master back on to his horse. Then the
two of them rode away in search of high
adventure.

THE GIANT'S LOVE SONG

Oh my love's enormous, just like me,
And just like me, she's true
And her eyes are like two basketballs
If basketballs were blue.

When my darling whispers in my ear
It is like a blunderbuss
And my love is dainty to be seen
As St Pancras Terminus.

Oh her face is like the scarlet sun
When the tropical sunset falls
And her breast is like Mount Everest
And her dome is like St Paul's.

Yes, her hair is like a forest fire,
Like a glowing tower her nose
And her teeth stand in her mighty gums
Like tombstones in two rows.

Like a nuclear power station, she
Is refined and glamorous
And she tiptoes o'er the dewy lawn
Like a double-decker bus.

Oh her knees are like two pyramids
When she's lying very still
And her foot is like a river barge
And her bottom's like Primrose Hill.

Oh my love's at least one hundred times
As big and fair as you.
Yes, my love's enormous, just like me,
And just like me, she's true.

The Sad Boy who Conquered the Giants

Long, long ago, before the white people came to Canada, there was a sad boy who lived with his uncle beside a dark forest. His uncle hated the boy's sadness, and longed to be rid of him.

The boy was sad because his mother and father were dead, and because his uncle cursed him and beat him and made him work until he dropped. The boy would have run away, but he was afraid to wander alone in the dark forest.

One day the sad boy's uncle heard that three giants had come to live in the forest.

Where they came from, nobody knew, but they lived in a great cave near the sea. They stole everybody's stores of food and ate up all the little children they could catch.

The Chief of the territory sent his best warrior to the cave to fight the giants. But next morning a piece of birch bark bearing a picture of the warrior with an arrow in his heart was found at the Chief's door, and the warrior never returned.

All the Chief's warriors were killed in the same way, and it seemed that nobody could stop the giants. All the country was in great terror.

The Chief called a great meeting and said: "I will give my own daughter to the man who can rid me of these giants."

Now the wicked uncle was at the meeting. He knew that the Chief had a ferocious temper and hated people who boasted. "I know how I'll get rid of this sad boy," he said to himself. "I'll tell the Chief that the boy claims he can kill any giant."

So he held up the sad boy's hand and said loudly: "Great Chief, this boy boasts that he can free your land from all the giants."

The Chief was surprised when he looked at the little boy. He said: "You have promised you can rid my land of giants. If you can do it, you may marry my daughter. If you fail, you will die. If you escape from the giants, I will kill you myself, for I hate idle boasters."

The sad boy went and sat by the ocean and cried like a small waterfall in springtime. He thought he was bound to die, for he was very small and didn't know how to kill anything, let alone a giant.

But as he sat there a wise old woman came along. She appeared very quietly and rapidly out of the grey mists of the sea. And she said to him: "Why are you crying, boy?"

The boy said: "I am crying because I have to kill the giants in that cave. And if I can't kill them I shall surely die."

But the Woman of the Mist, who was the kindly spirit of the sea, said to him: "Take this bag and this knife and these three little stones. Go tonight to the cave of the giants and use these things as I shall tell you, and all shall be well."

She gave the sad boy three small white stones and a little knife and a bag like the bladder of a bear. And she taught him how to use them. Then she disappeared into the grey mists which hung low on the ocean, and the boy never saw her again.

The boy lay down on the soft sands and fell asleep. When he awoke, the full moon was shining. Far along the coast in the silver light he could see a dark opening in the rocks. He knew it was the entrance to the cave of the giants.

Taking his bag and his knife and his three little stones, he walked towards it with a trembling heart. When he reached the mouth of the cave he could hear the giants snoring inside, louder than a stormy sea.

Then he remembered what the wise old woman had told him to do. He tied the bag inside his coat so the mouth of it was near his chin. Then he took one of the small stones from his pocket.

At once it grew to an enormous size, so heavy that the boy could hardly hold it. He threw it at the biggest giant and it hit him squarely on the forehead. The giant sat up, staring wildly and rubbing his brow.

Then he kicked his younger brother, who was lying beside him, and shouted angrily: "Why did you hit me?"

"I didn't hit you," said his brother.

"You bashed me on the head while I was asleep," said the biggest giant. "If you do it again, I'll kill you." Then the giants went back to sleep.

The boy took a second small stone from his pocket. It grew, and he hurled it at the biggest giant. The giant sat up, rubbed his head, then took a great axe and killed his brother with one blow. Then he went back to sleep.

The boy took the third stone, it grew and
he threw. The biggest giant sat up and
shouted: "Both my brothers have been
plotting to kill me!" He picked up his axe,
killed his other brother and went back to
sleep.

The sad boy gathered up the three stones, which were now small again, and slipped out of the cave.

Next morning, when the giant went to fetch water from the stream, the boy hid in a tree and began to cry loudly. The giant soon found him and asked: "Why you are crying, sad boy?"

"I have lost my way," said the boy, "My parents have gone and left me. Please let me be your servant. I would like to work for such a kind and handsome man."

Now the giant was fond of eating children, but he thought: "Now I am alone, I ought to have a companion. So I will spare this boy's life and he can be my servant." He took the boy back to his cave and said: "Cook my dinner before I come home. Make a pot of good stew, for I shall be very hungry."

The giant went off into the dark forest

while the boy prepared the evening meal. He cut up a great store of deer meat and put it in a huge pot and cooked it over a blazing fire all day.

When the giant came home that evening he was very hungry and well pleased to see such a good meal. He sat down one side of the pot and the boy sat the other, and they both dipped in their spoons.

The sad boy said: "We must eat up every scrap so that I can clean the pot ready for corn mush for our breakfast." The stew was very very hot, and to cool it before he ate it, the giant blew on the first spoonful.

But the boy poured his own spoonfuls into the bag under his coat, and he said scornfully: "Can't you eat hot food? A big man like you! In my country even a child doesn't stop to cool his food with his breath, but swallows it down like a warrior."

The giant was shortsighted and the cave was dark, so the giant couldn't see that the boy was pouring stew into a bag. He gulped down the hot stew and burned his mouth and his throat very badly. But he was too proud to stop or to complain.

When they had eaten half the potful, the giant said: "I'm full up. That's enough."

"Oh, no," said the boy, "you must show you like my cooking. In my country even a child eats more than that." The giant was not to be out-eaten by a boy, so he ate and ate until the pot was empty.

The boy had poured his share into the bag, and now it swelled out his coat to a great size. The giant could hardly move, he had eaten so much, and he said: "I'm full to bursting. I've got an awful belly-ache."

"Me too," said the boy, "but I know how to cure it." So he took his little knife and thrust it gently into the side of the bag, and

the stew oozed out and he was soon back to his normal size.

The giant stared in wonder, but the boy said: "That's what we always do in my country after a great feast."

"Doesn't it hurt?" asked the giant.

"Oh no," said the boy, "it makes you feel much better."

The giant felt so swollen and bloated that he could bear it no longer. So he took his own long knife. "Strike hard," said the boy, "or it'll do no good." The giant plunged his knife into his own stomach, and fell forward, dead, on the floor of the cave.

Then the boy took the stones and the bag and the knife which the Woman of the Mist had given him, and went and told the Chief what he had done. When the Chief had made sure that this was true and that the three giants were dead, he said to the boy: "You may have my daughter as your wife."

But the boy said: "I do not want your daughter. She is too old, and too fat. I only want traps to catch fish and animals." So the Chief gave the boy many good traps, and he went into a far country to be a hunter. And there he lived happily all by himself.

His wicked uncle never saw him again. And the land was never again troubled by giants, because of what the sad boy had done.

I am Boj

(to be shouted, in the voice of a terrible giant, at children who wake early in the morning)

I am Boj

I crackle like the Wig of a Judge

I am Boj

My eyes boil over with Hodge-Podge

I am Boj

Organized Sludge and a Thunder-Wedge

I am Boj

I am a Tower of solid Grudge

I am Boj

The molten Centre, the cutting Edge

I am Boj

From blackest Dudgeon I swing my Bludgeon

I am Boj

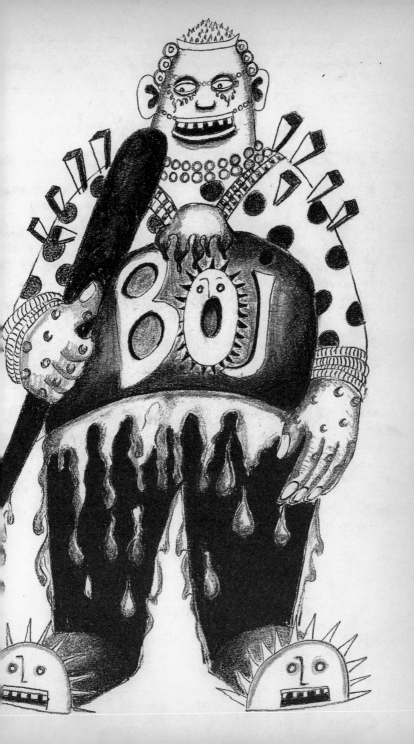

The Haunted Well

There was once a young man in India called Ram Singh who had been taught to speak truthfully but kindly to all people.

One day Ram Singh set out to seek his fortune.

On the road he encountered a great procession. There were servants and

attendants, soldiers, mule-drivers, camel-
drivers, merchants, singers and musicians,
as well as elephants, camels, horses, mules,
ponies, donkeys, goats, carts and wagons -
so that it seemed like a large town on the
march.

This was the company which escorted a great Rajah as he travelled through the land. Ram Singh went to the Rajah's chief Wazir and asked if he could journey with the party. The Wazir liked the young man and made him his own personal servant. They all travelled for days, till they entered a country which was like a sea of sand, where swirling dust floated in clouds and men and animals were half-choked by it. But when they halted at a village, every throat dusty with thirst, the local headmen said there was no water to be had. There was not a spring nor a well in all that place.

The Wazir was afraid when he heard this news, for that great company could not live three days without water. But then one old man spoke up and said: "Sir Wazir, there is one well of water only one mile away. It was made by a king hundreds of years ago. You have to follow a long flight of stone steps down into the dark depths of the earth to find that water. But nobody goes near it, because it is haunted by an evil spirit of a giant. Whoever goes down to that well is never seen again."

The Wazir stroked his beard and considered this. Then he turned to Ram Singh, who stood behind his chair. "There is a proverb," said the Wazir, "that no man can be trusted till he has been tried. Go and get the Rajah and his people water from this well."

So Ram Singh fastened two large brass jars to a mule and two smaller ones to his shoulders and set out with the old man for a guide. Soon they came to a ruined building with stone steps leading down into darkness. And there Ram Singh was left alone with his mule.

He tied up the animal and took up the four brass jars. He began to walk down the

steps into the darkness. They were broad white slabs of alabaster, which gleamed in the shadows as he went lower and lower.

Silence. Even the sound of his bare feet on the steps seemed to echo. Still he walked downwards into the dark.

At last Ram Singh reached a wide pool of sweet water. He washed his jars out carefully and then filled them. He took up the two smaller jars and began to climb the stairway.

But as his foot touched the lowest stair, he heard a noise as if the roof was collapsing. He looked up and saw a great giant standing staring at him.

In one hand the giant held a lamp which cast great shadows round the walls. In the other hand he held, clasped to his chest, a skeleton.

The giant looked wildly at the young man.

Then he said: "What do you think, O mortal one, of my fair and lovely wife?" And he held his lantern so that it shone upon the heap of white bones in his arms and he looked down at those bones most lovingly.

For the giant once had a very beautiful wife, whom he loved most dearly. When she died, he refused to believe she was dead, but always carried her about with him, even after she became nothing but bones.

Ram Singh did not know this, of course. But he did remember what he had been taught: to speak truthfully but kindly to all people. So he said:

"Truly, sir, I am sure there is nowhere you could find such another."

The giant was delighted. "Ah, you have good eyes!" he said. "I do not know how often I have killed those who insulted her by saying she was nothing but a heap of dry bones. You are a fine young man and I will help you."

He laid down the skeleton with great care and snatched up the big bronze jars full of water, carrying them up the steps and hitching them on to the mule before Ram Singh could reach the open air with the smaller jars.

"You have pleased me very much," said the giant. "And you may ask me any favour. Perhaps you would like me to show you where the treasure of the dead kings is buried?"

But Ram Singh shook his head. "I would ask you this favour, good giant," he said. "Leave off haunting this well so that people may fetch its water in peace."

The giant smiled and nodded. As Ram Singh rode away with his precious burden of water, he saw the giant striding away across the sands with his dead wife's skeleton in his arms.

The Rajah and the Wazir and all the
people and animals of the great caravan
rejoiced when Ram Singh returned with the
water. But he never said anything about his
adventure with the giant. He simply told
the Rajah that from now on everybody
could use the well. And everybody did use
it, and the well never ran dry, and the giant
was never seen again.

AT MIDNIGHT

I was listening, my sweet,
To my baby's heartbeat
And the whispering of her rattle
So I missed the thud
Through the mud and blood
Of the giants marching to battle.

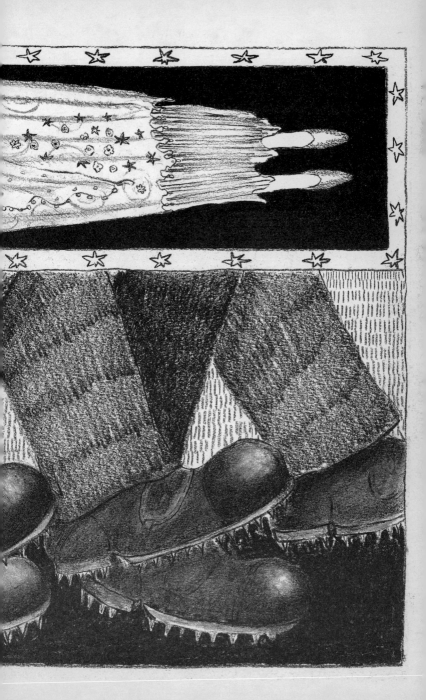

Bala of the Golden Lake

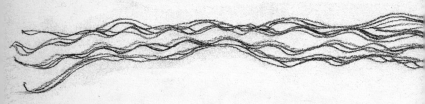

At the centre of the earth there is a great lake called Galana, whose waters are gold as April sunlight. And in that lake lives a beautiful giant called Bala. She has deep blue skin and snow-white hair and she lies in the lake waters dreaming, with only her head above the golden ripples.

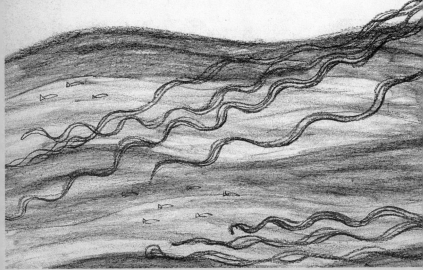

She is so big and peaceable that many people came to live in her hair, and they were called the Forest Tribe of Bala.

And other people came to stay inside her left ear and inside her right ear, and they were called the Wax Folk of Bala.

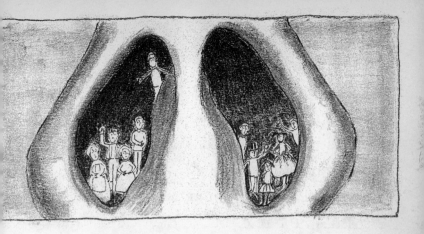

Others came and settled in her two nostrils, and they were known as the Sniff People of Bala.

Even more people came, and they decided to make their homes in her mouth, between her teeth and under her tongue, and they called themselves the Damp Nation of Bala.

So long as they sang and danced and cooked and grew crops, Bala didn't mind these people. They tickled a little, but they did her no harm, so she let them be and continued her dreaming.

But one day a breeze blew across the lake of Galana. The leaders of the Forest Tribe declared that everyone should move southwards, to the left and right ears of Bala, which would be much more sheltered.

The Wax Folk said there was no room, so the Forest Tribe invaded. The Wax Folk defended their caves fiercely. A bitter battle raged all down the bridge of the nose of Bala.

The sounds of battle echoed in the hairy caves of the Sniff People. The President of the Sniffs ordered everybody to take up arms and fight to defend the glorious nostrils of home.

Soon the Sniff People were fighting both the Forest Tribe and the Wax Folk at the same time, all along the soft slopes of the upper lip of Bala.

It was a terrible war and many injured and frightened people from the Forest Tribe, the Wax Folk and the Sniff People fled between the lips of Bala.

Then the Admiral of the Damp Nation fired a cannon and the Damp Navy set sail to get rid of the intruders. They chased them out through the lips and into battle.

By now the war was raging all over Bala's head. There were slashing swords and ferocious fires and shattering shells. And little streams of blood joined together to form a great crimson river.

Bala's hair was smouldering and her ears were aching and her nose was bleeding and her mouth was swollen and her eyes were covered in blood.

She reached down into the gold lake and took a handful of silver sand and rubbed it into her hair like shampoo. Then she took a deep breath and lowered her head under the waters of the lake.

She held her breath for a long time. She washed her hair, her ears and her nostrils. Then she came to the surface of the water.

She swilled out her mouth and spat.

Bala felt clean again. All the people had vanished from her head. Some, especially those in armour or in tanks, had sunk to the bottom of the lake. Others had swum away to land on the banks of the lake and begin the long journey to the surface of the earth.

Bala sighed and shook her wet hair. Then she lay back in the golden waters and continued her long dreaming.

(In North Wales, to this day, there is a lovely lake which bears her name.)

THE SADNESS OF A GIANT CHILD

I'm three years old.
I'm eight feet high.
They take me to a nursery school
And leave me to cry.

The grown-ups laugh.
The children scream.
I feel like a hairy
Monster in a dream.

Our teacher is a Tiny.
We call her Miss Priscilla.
Her favourite fairy story
Is Jack The Giant-Killer.

I sit in the corner
Like a wardrobe and sulk.
The other kids call me
The Incredible Hulk.

And the only time they let me
Join in a game
Is when I let them use me
As a climbing frame.

So each night I pray
To the God of the Tall:
"Please, Lord, let me
Grow up to be Small."

Seven at a Blow

Once upon a time there was a little tailor called Oliver, with spindly legs, gold-rimmed spectacles perched on the end of his nose and a scrawny neck.

One day, after a meal of raspberry pancakes, his table was covered with flies. So he hit at them with a heavy woollen sock. And when he looked at the sock, there were seven dead flies stuck to it with raspberry jam.

So he made himself a great leather belt. And on its buckle he wrote in words of silver: SEVEN AT A BLOW. Then Oliver set out to see the world.

The first person he met was a raggy boy, who sold him a sparrow. Oliver put it in his knapsack and went on his way.

The next person he met was a blue-eyed farmer's daughter, who sold him a piece of rich cream cheese. Oliver popped it in his knapsack and went on his way.

But then a shadow fell across the road. And the road began to tremble under Oliver's spindly legs. And he looked up fearfully, and there stood a giant, as big as ten Olivers.

The giant looked at the little tailor's belt and he saw the silver words: SEVEN AT A BLOW. He gasped. "Have you really killed seven with one blow?" asked the giant.

"Of course I have," said Oliver. "It was easy."

So the giant said: "Why don't we two have a trial of strength? I'll throw up a stone, and it won't come down for an hour."

Oliver said: "I'll throw up a stone, and it won't come down at all."

So the giant squashed up his arm muscles and threw a stone. One hour later, the stone landed on the road.

The tailor took the sparrow out of his pocket and let it soar up into the air like a flying stone. And of course it didn't come back again.

The giant was impressed, but he remembered a rhyme his dear old mother had taught him: "Don't give up, my little pup". So he said: "Let's have another test. Watch me crush this stone to powder."

The giant squashed up his finger muscles and crumbled the stone like a piece of stale bread and all that was left was white powder on the roadside.

Oliver said: "Watch me squeeze water out of this stone." He took his cream cheese and squeezed it till the water oozed out of it.

"You win," said the giant. "You're the strongest man I ever did meet."

They walked on together till they came to a tree laden with shining red cherries and the cherries were ripe. So the tailor climbed up the tree and began to pick.

But the giant bent down the top of the tree and sucked the cherries off the branches in bunches and spat out the leaves and twigs. When he'd finished, he let go.

The tree sprang back and Oliver was hurled high into the air. Luckily for him he fell on a pile of hay in the meadow.

He picked himself up and said: "Lucky I can fly so well. Otherwise I'd have broken my spindly legs, my gold-rimmed spectacles and my scrawny neck."

"Can you really fly?" asked the giant. "Oh, I wish I could fly. Won't you teach me how?"

"All right," said the tailor, "one of these days I'll teach you to fly."

So they walked on together again and came to a frightened town. A dragon had made his home in the church and was taking people in twos and threes, cooking them on its fiery breath and then eating them with onions.

The king had offered a thousand pounds and his daughter's hand in marriage to whoever could kill the dragon. So Oliver and the giant told the king that they would

kill the dragon.

When they came to the church door, the tailor stood back and said to the giant: "After you, my friend. If he sees my belt saying SEVEN AT A BLOW, the dragon will run away."

So the giant went in first and the dragon leapt upon him. And the giant and the dragon fought a terrible battle for seven days and seven nights. While they were fighting, Oliver sat in the church porch enjoying the food and drink which were brought by the townspeople. They all gasped when they read the words SEVEN AT A BLOW.

On the seventh night the giant finally killed the dragon and staggered out of the church. "I've done it!" he shouted. "I've killed the monster. And it's all because my dear old mother told me - Don't give up, my little pup."

But Oliver frowned at the giant. "You shouldn't have killed him," he said. "I wanted to take the dragon alive. We could have shown him at fairs and made tens of thousands of pounds."

"I'm very sorry," said the giant.

"All right," said Oliver. "You were quite brave. I'll tell you what - I'll teach you how to fly."

The giant was thrilled. So the tailor and the giant climbed up the tall steeple of the church.

"You must flap your arms seven times," said Oliver. "Then I'll say one, two, three - and you must jump."

"Just a little practice," said the giant, and he tried a few arm-flaps while muttering under his breath: "Don't give up, my little pup."

The tailor shook hands with him. "Right!" he said. "One, two, three - jump." The

giant flapped, the giant
jumped and the giant
broke his great neck on
the pavement far below.

Oliver climbed down
and told the King that
the dragon and the
giant had killed each
other. So the King
gave the little tailor
the thousand
pounds reward.

"Just one other thing, your majesty," said the little tailor. "What about marrying your daughter, the Princess Alicia?"

Now the Princess Alicia had been watching the little tailor ever since he arrived in the town. She didn't like his spindly legs nor his gold-rimmed spectacles nor his scrawny neck. And she didn't like his behaviour one bit.

Princess Alicia happened to be ten feet tall, and she liked the giant far more than Oliver. She would have married the giant gladly.

So she walked up to the little tailor and she turned him around and she kicked him all the way down the palace steps. And that palace has seven hundred and seventy-seven steps.

THREATENING

We have come to kill you, giant, we said,
To kill you and save this land.
He raised us up level with his head
On the palm of his table-size hand.

We looked deep into the giant's eye
It shone like a sunlit, blue-black lake
And its corners crinkled with laughter
And the giant's hand began to shake.

You have come to kill me, my little beans?
I'm the baby of the band -
For I stand on the hand of one ten times my size
And she stands on a bigger hand.

The Playful Giant
of Carn Galva

Every evening Morvah, the kind old giant,
would lay himself down on his great
rocking-stone and rock himself to sleep as
he watched the seagulls flocking and the
red sun going down into the sea off the
Cornish coast.

Near this logan-stone at Carn Galva, you
can still see the big, squarish rocks which
Morvah used as a child plays with wooden
bricks - building towers and knocking them
down for fun.

He protected the local people from bad
giants. Everybody loved him. His best

friend was a young man from Choon, who would walk over now and then for a chat and a game of quoits or hide-and-seek.

One afternoon these two friends had passed a cheerful afternoon together. As the young man put down his quoit to go home, the giant tapped him on the top of the head playfully with the tip of one finger.

"Come again tomorrow, my son, and we'll have a great game of hide-and-seek." But before he'd finished saying "hide-and-seek" the young man fell to the ground. The giant's finger had broken his friend's skull.

Morvah tried to mend the little head with clay and heather, but it was smashed beyond repair and the young man was dead. Then the poor giant took the body in his arms and cried and moaned louder than the ocean on the rocks below.

"Oh my poor son, my son, why didn't they make the shell of your head stonger? It was soft as pie-crust and far too thin! How shall I live without you to play hide-and-seek and quoits with me?"

The giant of Carn Galva never smiled again. They say that Morvah died of a broken heart within seven days or seven weeks or seven years.

THE FLYING GIANTS

What in the whirling world of wonder
Is that thunderous rumbling thumping
Pounding over and under the ocean,
Ripping asunder the blue silk of the sky?

That's the sound of the dreaded Flying Giants,
Their great silver-feather, leather-bound wings
Beating the air as they travel together –
But you must never ask where to, or why?

Simpkin Smallstuff
and the Starmaiden

His father was bigger than the Moon. His mother was bigger than the Sun. And their baby was ten times as big as his mother on the day that he was born.

So his mother and father, to keep him in order, called him Simpkin Smallstuff.

The day after he was born, Simpkin Smallstuff hauled up his nappy, which was woven from spacecloth. He decided to go for a walk through the Milky Way.

His head stuck up way beyond Bikkati, which is the furthest-up star you can imagine. His feet stood on the shell of the great tortoise of Dupooloo, who is as low down as it is possible to get.

Simpkin Smallstuff smiled. He had seen a beautiful sweetie spinning in the darkness. It was beautifully blue and white and green.

He reached out a few million miles with his chubby hands. He was just about to pick the bright round sweetie out of space and pop it into his gynormous mouth.

That would have been the end of this story and the end of you and me, for that shining sweetie was the Earth, our planet.

A Starmaiden was gliding by the Earth,

and she heard a singing from Africa and she sang the African song. And Simpkin Smallstuff's feet began to stamp out the rhythm.

Then the Starmaiden heard a singing from America, and she sang an American song. And Simpkin Smallstuff's feet changed their beat to match the new music.

So it went. The Starmaiden listened to songs from China and Scotland and Chile and Malaysia and Georgia and France and Mexico and Finland and India and New Zealand and Cyprus. And she sang these Earth songs aloud, and Simpkin Smallstuff danced and stomped on the back of the great tortoise of Dupooloo.

And so it still goes on, and the enormous baby has quite forgotten about eating the Earth.

Moral: We had better all keep singing, or Simpkin Smallstuff will eat us up.

Second Moral: Life is tough on tortoises.

HAIRY GIANTS

The hair that grows
On a giant's toes
Is bendable bulrushes
But the hair that grows
In a giant's nose
Is grisly bramble-bushes.